DO

CW01604763

This edition produced for The Book People Ltd, Hall Wood Avenue, Haydock, St Helens, WA11 9UL
BBC CHILDREN'S BOOKS
Published by the Penguin Group
Penguin Books Ltd, 80 Strand, London, WC2R 0RL, England
Penguin Group (USA) Inc., 375 Hudson Street, New York, New York 10014, USA
Penguin Books (Australia) Ltd, 250 Camberwell Road, Camberwell, Victoria 3124, Australia.
(A division of Pearson Australia Group Pty Ltd)
Canada, India, New Zealand, South Africa
Published by BBC Children's Books, 2007
Text and design © Children's Character Books, 2007
Written by Stephen Cole
10 9 8 7 6 5 4 3 2 1
BBC and logo © and TM BBC 1996. Doctor Who logo © BBC 2004. TARDIS image © BBC 1963.
Dalek image © BBC/Terry Nation 1963. Licensed by BBC Worldwide Limited.
DOCTOR WHO, TARDIS and DALEK and the DOCTOR WHO, TARDIS and DALEK logos are trade marks of the British Broadcasting Corporation and are used under licence.
ISBN-13: 978-1-85613-128-5
Printed in Great Britain by Clays Ltd, St Ives plc

DOCTOR WHO

QUIZ BOOK 3

CONTENTS

THE SIDEKICK FACTOR

The Doctor only ever takes the best with him on his travels through time and space... With a life as fast and furious as his, he can't afford to have anyone slowing him down! Try the test below and see if you have companion potential...

1. You find yourself unexpectedly on the moon when a moment ago you were safe and sound on Earth. Do you:

a) Find someone who knows what they're talking about and demand to be taken home at once.

b) Hide away and pretend none of it's happening.

c) Try to stay calm and reason out your situation – perhaps you can find a way to reverse it?

2. You find yourself being kidnapped by aliens who take off in a car. Do you:

a) Yell at them as loudly as possible and bully them into letting you go.

b) Grab one of the aliens' guns and pretend you will use it if they don't stop the car.

c) Signal to other motorists for help.

3. **The TARDIS lands on a strange planet on which the Doctor needs to run an errand. 'I won't be long,' he says, 'stay here until I get back.' Two hours pass and he does not return. Do you:**

a) Wander off to explore a bit while you're waiting.

b) Stay put – what's two hours? He'll be back soon.

c) Set off after him – he might be in trouble...

4. **You are woken in the dead of night by a terrifying scream. Do you:**

a) Yell at whoever's screaming to shut up and go back to bed.

b) Go and get the Doctor.

c) Run off to see if you can help whoever's screaming.

5. The Doctor takes you centuries back in time to see the Earth of another age. Do you:

a) Try to talk using old-fashioned language in an attempt to fit in with the locals.

b) Stand back and let the Doctor do the talking – he's the expert.

c) March around like you own the place, keeping your eyes and ears open.

6. Alone and defenceless on a strange world, you are being chased through thick fog by a savage, unknown creature. Do you:

a) Yell for help as you run.

b) Turn to fight the creature, pretending you are armed with a deadly weapon.

c) Stand still at the side of the street and hope it rushes past you in the fog.

7. In the middle of an exciting adventure, the Doctor starts babbling a particularly complicated explanation at you. Do you:

a) Whack him round the face to shut him up and tell him to speak slowly.

b) Nod and pretend you understand what he's on about - you don't want to seem stupid.

c) Try and re-phrase his explanations in your own words.

8. The Doctor is so intent on dealing with an enemy, the place around you is going up in smoke. Do you:

a) Drag him away before you both fry.

b) Scout out the quickest and safest route back to the TARDIS so you can make a quick getaway.

c) Point out the danger you're both in, in case he's overlooked it.

9. The Doctor offers to take you home. Do you:

a) Jump at the chance.

b) Suspect he secretly wants to dump you and agree, hiding your true feelings.

c) Tell him to get knotted – you love travelling through time and space and you're not ready to push off yet!

HOW DID YOU SCORE?

MOSTLY As

Blimey, you're a little bit, er... What's a polite way of putting it? Assertive. Or in other words, bossy, brassy, loud and full-on! It sounds like you're not very at ease on alien worlds or in menacing situations, demanding to be taken away from them or for someone to help you out, and so missing out on a unique chance to broaden your horizons by the Doctor's side. But that's OK, you're still great fun with bags of character – you're just not cut out for TARDIS travel.

MOSTLY Bs

Remember Martha's student friend in the Royal Hope hospital, Julia – the one who went to pieces, and who the Doctor dismissed as being useless in less than a moment? Well, with your clear lack of confidence, you're in danger of acting more like her than like Martha. When you're on your own, your behaviour seems a little rash and risky – acting on impulse can get you into worse trouble. So long as the Doctor is around, you're prepared to leave things entirely to him; and while your faith in him is well judged, this doesn't make you much of a team. The Doctor doesn't mind being questioned – it often helps him focus his thinking. And he wants to be sure that anyone travelling with him knows what's at stake at any given time – his world is too dangerous to have it any other way.

MOSTLY Cs

You demonstrate the same kind of easy common sense and self-awareness as Martha Jones. You aren't afraid to look stupid if it means getting things straight in your own mind, and you believe in taking positive steps to make things happen instead of hanging around and waiting for the Doctor to sort everything out. You may not always make the right decision, but you think things through before you act... and you're confident enough in your own abilities to be a real asset to the Doctor, someone he can plan with and confide in – well done!

THE RUNAWAY BRIDE
TRUE OR FALSE?

For Donna Noble, a fairytale Christmas wedding became a nightmare as she found herself at the centre of a terrifying, world-threatening alien plot... But did you look up from your presents long enough to even notice? Prove it by saying whether the statements below are true or false.

1. **Donna was transported from Earth into the TARDIS.**

   TRUE/FALSE

2. **She was getting married on Christmas Day.**

   TRUE/FALSE

3. **The Doctor took her straight back to the church where she was getting married.**

   TRUE/FALSE

4. **A robotic Santa kidnapped Donna and the Doctor chased them in the TARDIS.**

   TRUE/FALSE

5. **The robot Santas were working for the Empress of the Racnoss.**

TRUE/FALSE

6. **The Empress was bright blue.**

TRUE/FALSE

7. **She wanted to free her millions of children from the centre of the Earth.**

TRUE/FALSE

8. **The Doctor helped her.**

TRUE/FALSE

9. **The Empress perished when the Webstar was destroyed.**

TRUE/FALSE

10. **Donna and the Doctor had Christmas dinner together.**

TRUE/FALSE

ANSWERS:

1. True, 2. False, 3. False, 4. True, 5. True, 6. False, 7. True, 8. False, 9. True, 10. False.

SCORES:

8-10 Should the children of the Racnoss ever return, you will be ready for them.

5-7 Did you doze off a bit after Christmas lunch? Shame on you!

0-4 Looks like Huon particles have eaten away your brain — unlucky!

MEET MARTHA

Martha Jones was hurled headlong into the Doctor's life after an incredible lunar adventure... but how well have you got to know her since? Take the test and see!

1. How old is Martha?

a) 45.

b) 34.

c) 23.

2. What was Martha's occupation before she went off in the TARDIS?

a) Journalist.

b) Medical student.

c) Shop worker.

3. What is the name of Martha's sister?

a) Trisha.

b) Tish.

c) Sandra.

4. What family event ended messily shortly before the Doctor came back for Martha?

a) Her sister's 18th birthday party.

b) Her father's engagement party.

c) Her brother's 21st birthday party.

5. What was the first alien creature Martha bumped into?

a) A Slab.

b) A Judoon.

c) A Carrionite.

6. Where did Martha and the Doctor first meet?

a) On Earth.

b) On the Moon.

c) On New Earth.

7. Where did Martha go on her first journey into the past?

a) To see William Shakespeare.

b) To see Queen Victoria.

c) To see Henry VIII.

8. At which hospital did Martha work?

a) Royal Lancaster.

b) Royal Dutch.

c) Royal Hope.

9. **Martha's father had a trouble-making girlfriend called:**
   a) Annette.
   b) Annalise.
   c) Anaconda.

10. **How did the Doctor prove to Martha that he could travel in time?**
    a) He took her back to the sixteenth century.
    b) He collected Martha's great-great-great grandmother and brought her back to meet Martha.
    c) He went back into Martha's own past and spoke to her before they had actually met.

ANSWERS:

1. c, 2. b, 3. b, 4. c, 5. a,
6. a, 7. a, 8. c, 9. b. 10. c.

SCORES:

7-10 You must be one of Martha's biggest fans — and who can blame you!
4-6 Even Annalise would score more points than you! Well, maybe. . .
0-3 Were you one of Martha's patients and you're sulking because she left?!

SMITH AND JONES
TRUE OR FALSE?

Rain that falls upwards! Thuggish alien law–enforcers on the moon! Kidnapped hospitals! Bloodsucking old ladies! Some think this whole incredible lunar adventure was simply an illusion – but can you tell fact from fantasy?

Answer true or false to the statements below.

1. **The Doctor was investigating strange goings-on at a hospital by pretending to be a patient.**
   TRUE/FALSE
2. **He met Martha in the hospital basement to discuss his findings.**
   TRUE/FALSE
3. **The entire hospital was transported to Mars.**
   TRUE/FALSE
4. **The hospital was invaded by the Judoon.**
   TRUE/FALSE
5. **The Judoon were searching for a Plasmavore criminal.**
   TRUE/FALSE

6. **The Plasmavore was disguised as an old man.**
TRUE/FALSE

7. **It had assistants made from solid plastic.**
TRUE/FALSE

8. **The Doctor almost died when the Plasmavore sucked out his blood.**
TRUE/FALSE

ANSWERS:

1. True. 2. False. 3. False. 4. True. 5. True.
6. False. 7. False. 8. True.

SCORES

6-8 A score to put you over the moon as well as on it!

3-5 You know you can do better than this — perhaps you should go to Martha's old hospital for a check up?

0-2 It's Smith and Jones and Hopeless with you along for the ride!

NAME-DROPPER!

On the Doctor's endless travels he has met lots of famous people and been involved in many remarkable historical events. How much do you know about them?

1. **The Doctor says his coat was given to him by Janis Joplin. Who was she?**
   a) A famous hairdresser.
   b) A coat-maker.
   c) An American rock star.

2. **Which famous classical musician did the Doctor tell Martha he hung around with?**
   a) Mozart.
   b) Paul McCartney.
   c) Beethoven.

3. The Doctor reveals that Emmeline Pankhurst once stole his laser spanner. Who was she?

a) A tool thief.

b) An alien from Pankos.

c) A political activist who helped women win the right to vote.

4. The Doctor implies he flew a kite with Benjamin Franklin and got rope burns, soaked and electrocuted. This was no simple kite-flight – what was Franklin trying to prove?

a) That people can survive lightning strikes.

b) That kites can stay in the air in heavy rain.

c) That lightning is electricity.

5. According to Mickey Smith, the Doctor knew Cleopatra very well. What did he call her?

a) Patty.

b) Cleo.

c) Cleethorpes.

6. **The Doctor claims he almost lost his thumb when Skylab re-entered Earth's atmosphere in 1979. What was Skylab?**

a) The first satellite launched by the Soviet Union.

b) The first space station launched by the USA.

c) An asteroid.

7. **Which famous drink did the Doctor claim to invent at a party in the 18th century?**

a) The banana daiquiri.

b) The fruity fizzeroo.

c) Orange squash.

ANSWERS:

1. c, 2. c, 3. c, 4. c, 5. b, 6. b, 7. a.

SCORES

6-7 With a score as high as this, you could find people are soon name-dropping YOU!

3-5 Not a bad score — but you're clearly not famous for your great knowledge.

0-2 Sounds like you're INFAMOUS for getting quiz answers wrong — better luck next time!

THE VITAL LETTERS

There are many words hidden in the maze of letters below. Solve the clues, then ring each word as you find it. The words can go up or down, backwards or forwards and may overlap. The numbers in brackets tell you how many letters the word is. The letters left over spell out a name... what is it?

T	H	A	W	M	N
Y	B	A	A	O	A
N	O	C	L	O	M
C	E	S	C	N	U
G	L	O	B	E	H
A	A	R	C	A	M

1. **Professor Lazarus was funded by this wealthy Lady. (4)**
2. **The Judoon moved an entire hospital to the ____. (4)**
3. **The Face of ___. (3)**

4. The leader of the Cult of Skaro was Dalek ___. (3)

5. Martha's brother's first name. (3)

6. To hide from the Family of Blood, the Doctor made himself _____. (5)

7. These creatures lurked in the Undercity in New New York. (5)

8. Milo and Cheen's car was smashed about by the above creatures' giant ____s. (4)

9. The site of the Doctor's final battle with the Carrionites was the _____ Theatre. (5)

10. The sister planet of Raxacoricofallapatorius. (4)

T	H	A	W	M	N
Y	B	A	A	O	A
N	O	C	L	O	M
C	E	S	C	N	U
G	L	O	B	E	H
A	A	R	C	A	M

The name you can spell from the letters left over is YANA.

1. Thaw, 2. Moon, 3. Boe, 4. Sec, 5. Leo, 6. human, 7. Macra, 8. claw, 9. Globe, 10. Clom.

ANSWERS:

ODD ONE OUT

Look at the different groups of people, places and things below. In each case, which is the odd one out – and why?

1. Brannigan, Novice Hame, Sister Jatt, Valerie.

2. The Doctor, Morgenstern, Florence Finnegan, Martha Jones.

3. The Face of Boe, Captain Jack, Richard Lazarus, Cassandra.

4. Mr Stoker, Baines, Latimer, Hutchinson.

5. Gravitic anomaliser, helmic regulator, sonic screwdriver, handbrake.

6. Dr Rajesh Singh, Shakespeare, Captain Jack Harkness, the security guard at Alexandra Palace.

ANSWERS:

1. Valerie – the others are all Catkind.
2. Morgenstern – the others all registered as alien on the Judoon scanners.
3. Lazarus – the others have met both the Ninth and Tenth Doctors.
4. Mr Stoker – the others were all pupils at Farringham School in 1913.
5. Sonic screwdriver – the others are all parts of the TARDIS.
6. The security guard – the Doctor's psychic paper has failed to work properly on all the others.

SCORES:

5-6 Excellent reasoning. You could out-think a Dalek!

3-4 Not bad. If the Dalek was badly damaged and distracted by enemies, you might just out-think it.

1-2 Oh dear. You couldn't out-think a dead Dalek.

0 EXTERMINATE!

MONSTER ALERT!

The Doctor is never short of monstrous opponents... but how much do you know about the latest batch he's come up against? Take this terrifying test and find out...

1. Where did the Lazarus creature come from?

a) Mars.

b) Dormant genes in Lazarus's DNA.

c) A parallel Earth.

2. What creatures lurked in the fumes beneath the Undercity of New New York?

a) Cassandra and Chip.

b) The Face of Boe and Novice Hame.

c) The Macra.

3. What is the motto of the Judoon?

a) Justice is swift.

b) Justice will prevail.

c) Just hold still and we won't kill you.

4. **Which Dalek experimented on its own cells to introduce human elements?**
   a) Dalek Thay.
   b) Dalek Sec.
   c) Dalek Omega.

5. **What is the approximate lifespan of the Family of Blood?**
   a) Three months.
   b) Three years.
   c) Three weeks.

6. What is another name for the sinister statue-like Weeping Angels?

a) The Stone Biters.

b) The Lonely Assassins.

c) The Carved Killers.

7. Which phrase was uttered by the Sun-possessed on-board SS Pentallian?

a) Burn and die.

b) Burn with me.

c) Burn a sausage.

8. How can you tell Futurekind apart from human beings?

a) By their extra legs.

b) By their third eyes.

c) By their teeth.

ANSWERS:

1. b, 2. c, 3. a, 4. b, 5. a, 6. b, 7. b, 8. c

SCORES

7-8 You know your monsters... should you ever bump into one, you will be cool, calm and capable!

3-6 You know a bit about your monsters... should you ever bump into one, you will be nervous, but might just deal with it OK!

0-2 You know nothing about monsters, not even that there's one RIGHT BEHIND YOU!

GADGETS GALORE

In the Doctor's high-tech universe you can always depend on one thing – that there's an amazing gizmo for every occasion! Take the test below to see how gadget-minded you are...

1. Where are 'infected' victims placed on-board the SS Pentallian?

a) A tranquiller couch.

b) A stasis chamber.

c) A cryogenic bedroom.

2. What flavour of toothpaste did the Doctor's special travel toothbrush come loaded with?

a) Venusian spearmint.

b) Martian aniseed.

c) Raxacoricofallapatorian raspberry.

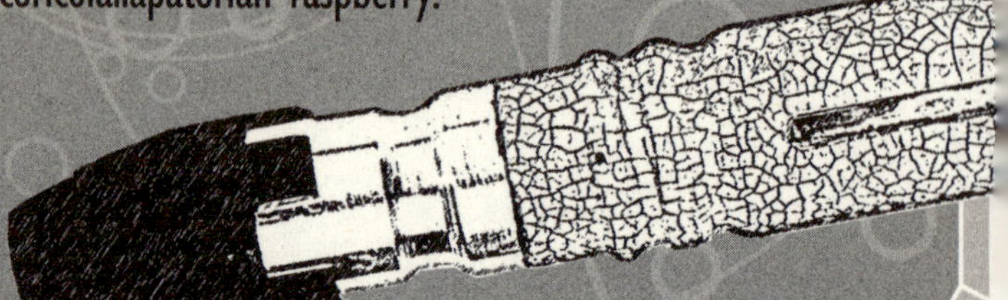

3. What did Lazarus use to destabilise his cell structure?

a) Hypersonic sound waves.

b) Supersonic radio waves.

c) A screwdriver.

4. To escape the Family of Blood, what does the Doctor use to rewrite his body chemistry?

a) A DNA transformer.

b) A chameleon arch.

c) A transmutation stimulator.

5. What does the Doctor give Donna to stop the robotic Santas from finding her?

a) A special ring that contains a bio-damper.

b) A wedding cake.

c) A special shielding veil.

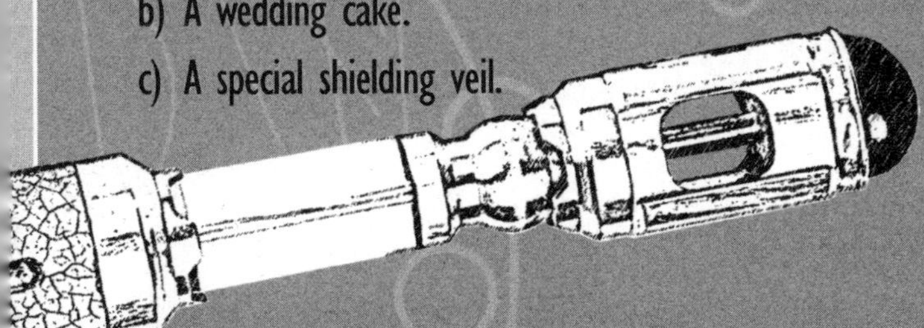

6. **What do the Judoon use to transport the Royal Hope hospital to the Moon?**
   a) An H_2O scoop.
   b) A levitation ray.
   c) A matter transmitter.

7. **What prevents John Smith from taking an interest in his mysterious fob watch?**
   a) A perception filter.
   b) A laser spanner.
   c) Electric shocks.

8. **What scientific process do the Family of Blood use to bring scarecrows to life?**
   a) Straw control.
   b) Stuffing reanimation.
   c) Molecular fringe animation.

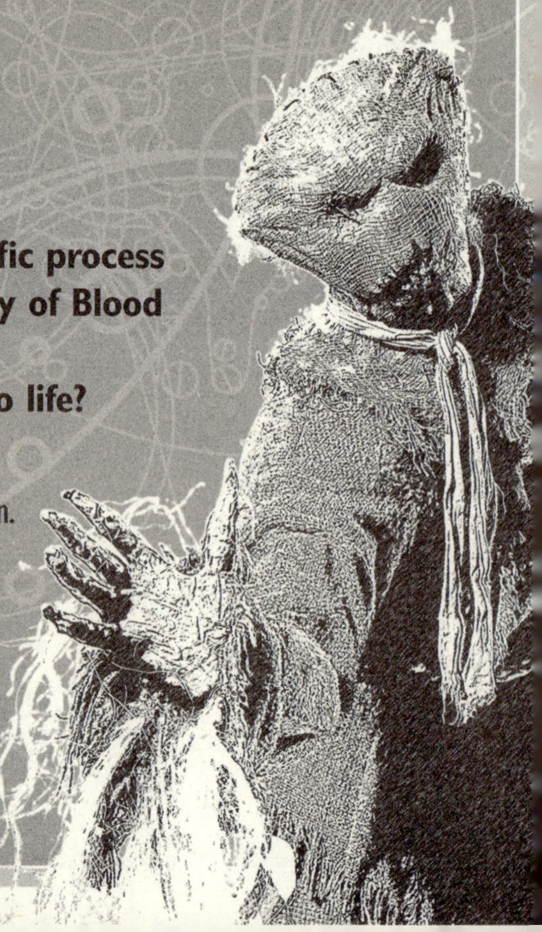

9. **When the TARDIS was dragged back to the Racnoss's underground base, what did the Doctor use to alter its landing site?**

a) The extrapolator.

b) A teaspoon.

c) A coordinate booster.

10. **What did Captain Jack use to travel back from the year 200,100 to the 19th century?**

a) A TARDIS.

b) A time ring.

c) A Vortex Manipulator.

ANSWERS:

1. b, 2. a, 3. a, 4. b, 5. a, 6. a, 7. a, 8. c, 9. a, 10. c.

SCORES

8-10 You've got a good eye for gadgets — in fact, you probably have visual implants!

5-7 Have you thought of fitting a brain booster to your head? It may help you get better marks next time!

0-4 Oh, dear, call your local mind-tech repair-bot — your brain is definitely on the blink!

THE SHAKESPEARE CODE

TRUE OR FALSE?

Dark forces are at work in the London of 1599... Alien creatures who wish to bring about a millennium of blood, using the genius of a very famous author. To answer true to the statements below, or to answer false? These are the questions!

1. **The Doctor and Martha decided to go to the Globe theatre to see a play.**
   TRUE/FALSE
2. **They met the famous author, Charles Dickens.**
   TRUE/FALSE
3. **William Shakespeare fancied Martha.**
   TRUE/FALSE
4. **An alien Carrionite compelled Shakespeare to include special words at the end of his new play.**
   TRUE/FALSE
5. **Once read aloud, these words would banish the human race into a black hole.**
   TRUE/FALSE

6. **The shape of the Globe theatre was designed to amplify the special words, allowing the Carrionites to enter our world.**
   TRUE/FALSE
7. **Shakespeare made up a short poem to close up the portal between the Carrionites' prison and the Earth.**
   TRUE/FALSE
8. **The Doctor and Martha chased away the Carrionites with broomsticks.**
   TRUE/FALSE

ANSWERS:

1. True. 2. False. 3. True. 4. True.
5. False 6. True. 7. True. 8. False.

SCORES:

6-8 Well done - you've cracked The Shakespeare Code!

3-5 If "All the world's a stage", it looks like you've forgotten some of your lines!

0-2 Oh dear - looks like your brain cells have gone the same way as Love's Labours Won!

GALLIFREY GUIDE

It's long since been destroyed, but the name Gallifrey lives on – known only to a few, spoken of in a hushed whisper... how much do you know about this fabled world that was once the Doctor's home?

1. What race lived on Gallifrey?

a) The Time Lords.

b) The Racnoss.

c) The Daleks.

2. What colour was the sky on Gallifrey?

a) Silver.

b) Blue.

c) Burnt orange.

3. If you could visit Gallifrey, on which continent would you find the Mountains of Solace and Solitude?

a) Ailartsua.

b) The continent of Wild Endeavour.

c) Dalekkos.

4. What mighty cathedral-like dwelling place would you find there?

a) The Time Lord Stadium.

b) The Space-Time car park.

c) The Citadel.

5. At what age were the children of Gallifrey taken from their families to enter the Academy?

a) Eight.

b) 800.

c) 80.

6. What name was given to the gap in the fabric of reality through which the Vortex of time and space could be seen?

a) The Untempered Schism.

b) The Split.

c) The Oncoming Storm.

7. What name was given to the apocalyptic battle between the Time Lords and the Daleks?

a) The Dalek-Time Lord War.

b) The Immense Conflict.

c) The Great Time War.

8. Apart from the Doctor, which other Time Lord survived the Time War?

a) Cassandra.

b) The Master.

c) The Nurse.

ANSWERS:

1. a, 2. c, 3. b, 4. c, 5. a, 6. a, 7. c, 8. b.

SCORES:

6-8 With a score like this, you could be a learned scholar of Gallifrey!

3-5 Time Lords are not supposed to interfere — otherwise we would tell you to study harder if you wish to excel in Time Lord knowledge.

0-2 Never mind 'Time Lord' — you are a 'Wrong Answer' Lord! Try harder to find out more about Gallifrey, then take the test again!

GRIDLOCK
TRUE OR FALSE?

New New York in the year five billion and fifty-three is a dangerous place – particularly if you venture near the fast lane of the motorway... How closely were you watching the Doctor and Martha's adventures there? Find out by taking the test below. Happy driving!

1) **The Doctor had never been to New New York before.**
   TRUE/FALSE

2) **The TARDIS landed in Pharmacy Town.**
   TRUE/FALSE

3) **Martha was kidnapped by Milo and Cheen, who took her away in their car.**
   TRUE/FALSE

4) **They wanted her to guide them to the upper levels of the motorway.**
   TRUE/FALSE

5) **Some people had been stuck in their cars on the motorway for over twenty years.**
TRUE/FALSE

6) **The Doctor followed Martha on a flying moped.**
TRUE/FALSE

7) **Milo and Cheen's car was attacked by giant monsters called Macra.**
TRUE/FALSE

8) **The Doctor had never seen Macra before.**
TRUE/FALSE

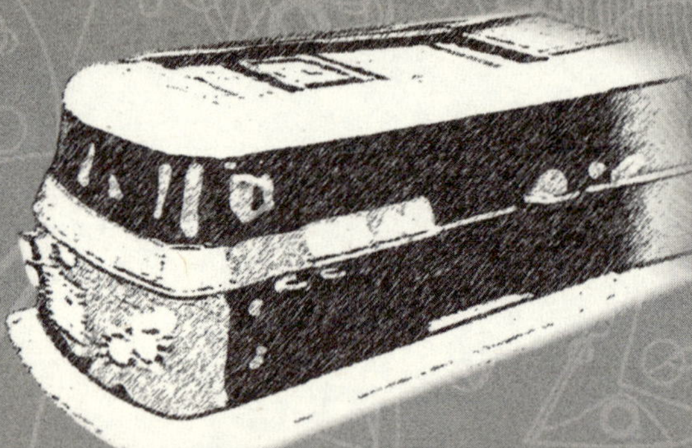

ANSWERS:

1. False 2. True 3. True 4. False 5. True 6. False 7. True 8. False.

SCORES:

6-8 When it comes to Doctor Who knowledge you're zooming along in the fast lane - just watch out for giant claws!

3-5 You're cruising along fine, but mind how you go - your engine's definitely spluttering a bit.

0-2 CRASH AND BURN! Have you been buying 'forget' patches from Pharmacy Town again?

SPACEBOUND

It's a big old universe out there... and the Doctor's met things from both its beginning and end. But how much do YOU know about deep space and beyond?

1. What is supposed to lie far beyond the Condensate Wilderness, out towards the Wildlands and the Dark Matter Reefs?

a) New Earth.

b) Sanctuary Base Three.

c) Utopia.

2. In which region of space was the SS Pentallion when the Doctor and Martha came on-board?

a) The Pacific Rim.

b) The Torajii System.

c) The Solar System.

3. Where would you find New New York?

a) New Earth.

b) New Mars.

c) Newton's World.

4. According to the Carrionites, "The light of Shadmock's hollow moon doth shine on to a point in space..."

a) Betwixt Dravidian Shores and Linear 5930167.02.
b) Where light is gobbled by the several elements.
c) Where no soul sleeps at the midnight hour.

5. What does a ship need in order to travel through space when there are no stars for guidance?

a) Pig Slaves.
b) A navigation matrix.
c) A Zeus plug.

6. How were the Master and the Toclafane planning to launch their war on the universe?

a) By contacting space region one.
b) By exploding a black hole at the centre of the universe.
c) By opening up a rift into Braccatolian Space.

7. Where was Professor Yana discovered as an orphan, apparently abandoned?

a) Earth.
b) The coast of the Silver Devastation.
c) The dark shores of the Malmooth.

8. What is the name of the Daleks' home planet?

a) Skaro.

b) Mondas.

c) Barcelona.

ANSWERS:

1. c, 2. b, 3. a, 4. a, 5. b, 6. c, 7. b, 8. a.

SCORES

7-8 You know your space facts.... almost too well! Are you an alien?

3-6 Not too bad - but with a score like this there's plenty of space to improve!

0-2 Looks like the space you know best is that large one between your ears! But if you pay dose attention to the Doctor's travels you could still be a star.

JACK IS BACK!

When the Doctor meets up with Captain Jack Harkness again, it marks the start of one of his most dangerous and exciting adventures. But how much do you know about everyone's favourite Captain...?

1. Which secret organisation does Captain Jack head up?

a) Firewood.
b) Torchwood.
c) Borehamwood.

2. What is special about Jack?

a) He's won the 'Galactic Hunk' award three times running.
b) He cannot be killed.
c) He's got three knees.

3. The last thing Captain Jack remembers of his 'mortal' life is:

a) Drinking a hyper-vodka with alien agents.
b) Seeing Rose Tyler fighting a Slitheen.
c) Facing three Daleks about to exterminate him.

4. What, according to Captain Jack, happened the first time he realized he could return from the dead?

a) He got into a fight on Ellis Island in 1892 and a man shot him through the heart.

b) He got into a laser fight on Space Station Gamma Zero in 200,100.

c) He was blown up in World War II.

5. What did Captain Jack do when he saw the Doctor taking off from Cardiff, trying to leave him behind?

a) He shot an alien weapon at the TARDIS.

b) He jumped on to the side of the TARDIS and clung on as it sped through the vortex.

c) He jumped on to the roof of the TARDIS and crawled inside through the roof hatch.

6. **Before entering the radiation chamber on Malcassairo, what did Captain Jack remove?**

a) A control linkage panel.

b) His top.

c) The Doctor's shoes.

7. **Who did Jack secretly watch growing up in the 1990s?**

a) Mickey Smith.

b) Rose Tyler.

c) Martha Jones.

8. **How did Jack destroy the Paradox Machine?**

a) With a machine gun.

b) With a Dalek gun.

c) With a laser screwdriver.

ANSWERS:

1. b, 2. b, 3. c, 4. a, 5. b, 6. b, 7. b, 8. a.

SCORES

7-8 When it comes to knowledge of Jack, you are clearly the Captain!

4-6 Hmm – perhaps you are experiencing some perception distortion? Hopefully when it passes, your score will improve!

0-3 You do remember Captain Jack, don't you? Handsome American guy, yeah? No? Hello. . . ?

EVOLUTION IN MANHATTAN

TRUE OR FALSE?

When the Doctor and Martha visit Manhattan in 1930, they are soon caught up in the terrifying schemes of the Daleks and their sinister servants. But how caught up were YOU in those incredible events?

1. **The Doctor and Martha went to Hooverville, where the unemployed of New York lived.**
   TRUE/FALSE
2. **People there had been going missing.**
   TRUE/FALSE
3. **Some of them were being turned into grotesque Pig Slaves by the Daleks.**
   TRUE/FALSE

4. **The Daleks had taken over a block of flats in Manhattan.**

   TRUE/FALSE

5. **The Daleks were conducting experiments to make themselves half-pig.**

   TRUE/FALSE

6. **Dalek Sec planned to convert specially-prepared slaves into a new Dalek breed.**

   TRUE/FALSE

7. **The Daleks built an energy conductor on top of the Empire State Building to accomplish their plans.**

   TRUE/FALSE

8. **The Doctor transmitted Martha's DNA into the Daleks' creations to stop them obeying without question.**

   TRUE/FALSE

ANSWERS:

1. True. 2. True. 3. True. 4. False. 5. False. 6. True. 7. True. 8. False.

SCORES

6-8 An excellent score - your brain must be highly evolved!

3-5 Perhaps if you stand near a blast of gamma lightning, you will evolve into something smarter!

0-2 READING BRAINWAVES... LOW INTELLIGENCE! THIS ONE WILL BECOME A PIG SLAVE!

MONSTER MERGE

Look at the hybrid monsters on the following pages and see if you can work out which aliens have merged to create them.

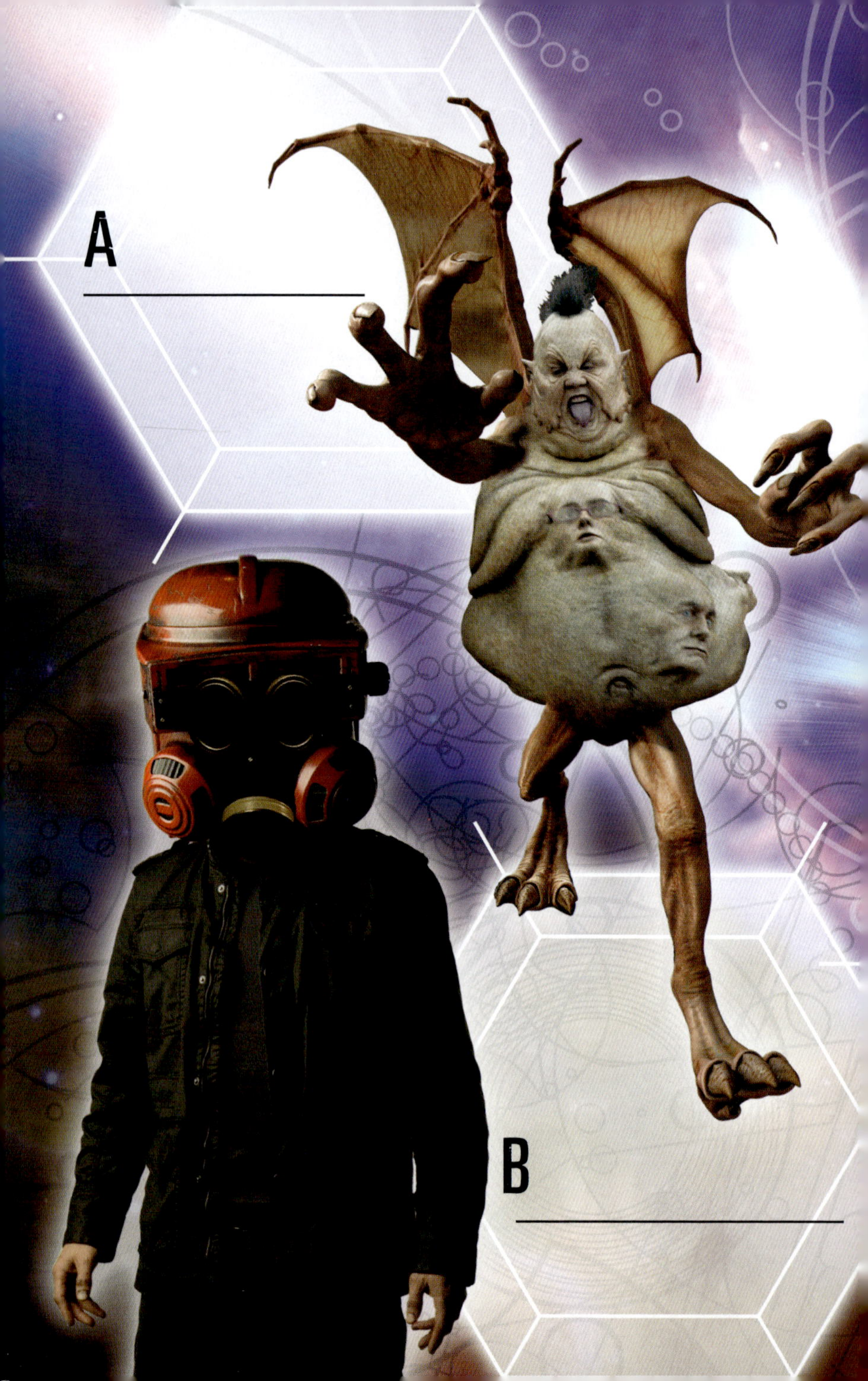
A
B

C

D

E

F

G

H

I
J

K

L

ANSWERS:

B. Sun-possessed and the Empty Child. D. A Slitheen and a Weeping Angel.

Krillitane and Abzorbaloff. C. The Lazarus monster and a Cyberman.

A Cyberman, an Ood and a Sycorax. G. A Clockwork robot and a 'pilot fish' robot.

F. The Judoon Captain and the Dalek Sec Hybrid. H. Chantho and a Pig Slave.

A Slitheen and the Jagrafess. K. Lilith and Florence, the Plasmavore.

J. The Werewolf and Novice Hame. L. Laszlo and Mother Doomfinger.

MASTER-MIND

How much do you know about the Doctor's sadistic, scheming arch-enemy? Take the terrible test below and find out... if you dare.

1. **When did the Master flee from the Time War?**
   a) When the first shot was fired.
   b) When he was called upon to fight in the Time Lord army.
   c) When the Dalek Emperor took control of the Cruciform.

2. How did the Master hide himself from the War?

a) He made himself human.

b) He jumped in a big hole.

c) He lived inside a hollowed-out asteroid on the edge of space.

3. What identity did the Master create for himself when he became human?

a) Professor Propitious.

b) Professor Yana.

c) Professor Doom.

4. Why did the Master regenerate on Malcassairo?

a) He was shot.

b) He wanted to have a younger body.

c) He was bombarded with lethal radiation.

5. What identity did the Master create for himself on Earth?

a) Harold Saxon.

b) Edward Viking.

c) Samson Churchill.

6. What was the name of the woman the Master made his wife and companion?

a) Jenny.

b) Dawn.

c) Lucy.

7. What was the name of the communications network launched by the Master?

a) Archangel.

b) Weeping Angel.

c) New Angel.

8. What is the name of the super-advanced aircraft carrier used by the Master as his base?

a) Valiant.

b) Strident.

c) Victory.

9. What incredible device did the Master create using the Doctor's TARDIS?

a) The Pandora Machine.

b) The Paradox Machine.

c) The Infinite Engine.

10. With which race did the Master ally himself?

a) The Toclafane.

b) The Judoon.

c) The Family of Blood.

11. The Master suspended the Doctor's ability to regenerate and aged him how far?

a) 10 years.

b) 500 centuries.

c) 900 years.

12. Where did the Master find the creatures he named the Toclafane?

a) Utopia.

b) Earth.

c) Woman Wept.

13. How did the Master finally die?

a) He was shot by Captain Jack.

b) He refused to regenerate after being shot.

c) The Toclafane destroyed him.

ANSWERS:

1. c, 2. a, 3. b, 4. a, 5. a, 6. c, 7. a, 8. a, 9. b, 10. a, 11. c, 12. a, 13. b.

SCORES:

11-13 An excellent score revealing extensive knowledge - you are the Master of this quiz all right!

7-10 Not bad at all - but perhaps your true masterly essence is sitting in a pocket watch hidden from you by a perception filter.

3-6 Oh dear - was the sound of intense drumming in your ears putting you off?

0-2 You are very definitely the Junior! Better luck next time.

THE LAZARUS EXPERIMENT
TRUE OR FALSE?

It's dangerous to mess around with nature, but this is a lesson that humans rarely learn. Richard Lazarus was one of them – and he found out the truth the hard way. Answer the true or false statements below to find out how much you remember!

1. **The TARDIS landed in a busy street.**
   TRUE/FALSE
2. **Martha's sister arranged for Martha to be invited to a special demonstration at Lazarus Laboratories.**
   TRUE/FALSE

3. **Richard Lazarus experimented on himself inside a special capsule.**
TRUE/FALSE

4. **He came back out looking much older.**
TRUE/FALSE

5. **The experiment activated something in Lazarus's DNA.**
TRUE/FALSE

6. **Lazarus's first victim was a young woman.**
TRUE/FALSE

7. **The Doctor tried to defeat the creature by blasting him with fire extinguishers.**
TRUE/FALSE

8. **He also attempted to defeat Lazarus by reversing the polarity of his capsule so that it reflected hypersonic energy.**
TRUE/FALSE

ANSWERS:

1. False. 2. True. 3. True. 4. False. 5. True 6. False. 7. False. 8. True.

SCORES:

6-8 A score worthy of a professor. Your mind is as sharp and wily as Lazarus's - but let's hope you don't end up like him!

3-5 A score worthy of a lab assistant. Your smartness gene could perhaps benefit from some minor manipulation.

0-2 A score worthy of someone who's just wandered into the lab with no knowledge of anything much - go back outside and don't come back till you've studied Lazarus more closely!

WHAT'S IN A NAME?

The Doctor and Martha have encountered so many memorable characters in so many amazing places it's a wonder they keep track of them all. How about you – are YOU good with names? This quiz will soon provide the answer!

1. **Who was Brannigan?**
   a) One of the Catkind on New Earth.
   b) A pupil at Farringham school.
   c) A surgeon at Royal Hope hospital.

2. **Who was Lance Bennett?**
   a) A soldier on board the Valiant.
   b) A crewmember on board SS Pentallion.
   c) Donna Noble's fiancé, who worked for the Empress of the Racnoss.

3. Who was Lady Thaw?

a) A close supporter of Professor Lazarus.

b) A teacher at Farringham school.

c) A pig slave.

4. Who was Solomon?

a) A crew member on board SS Pentallian.

b) The human absorbed by Dalek Sec.

c) The leader of Hooverville in 1930s New York.

5. Who was Mother Doomfinger?

a) A Plasmavore.

b) A Carrionite.

c) Shakespeare's housekeeper.

6. Who was Laszlo?

a) A young man turned into a pig slave.

b) An actor in Shakespeare's theatre company.

c) A human waiting to board the rocket to Utopia.

7. Who was D.I. Billy Shipton?

a) One of Harold Saxon's shady assistants.

b) A policeman investigating the disappearance of Donna Noble.

c) An admirer of Sally Sparrow sent into the past by the Weeping Angels.

8. Who was Kath McDonnell?

a) Captain of the SS Pentallian.

b) Tish Jones's best friend.

c) Professor Yana's lab assistant.

ANSWERS:

1. a, 2. c, 3. a, 4. c, 5. b, 6. a, 7. c, 8. a.

SCORES

7-8 An excellent score – you are clearly going to be making a name for yourself in Who quizzes!

4-6 Not bad, but no one will be mentioning your name in connection with Who experts.

0-3 Your name will be MUD unless you swot up on your Who knowledge pronto!

42

TRUE OR FALSE?

On a far-distant spaceship, the Doctor and Martha had a battle against the clock as well as against... But that would be telling! If you're a naturally bright, you'll be burning to tackle this true or false quiz!

1. **The TARDIS landed on a holiday ship that was taking tourists across the galaxy.**
   TRUE/FALSE

2. **The ship's engines were working perfectly.**
   TRUE/FALSE

3. **The ship was going to crash into the nearest sun.**
   TRUE/FALSE

4. **Martha and another crew member tried to reach a spare shuttle so everyone could get away.**
TRUE/FALSE

5. **The Doctor discovered that some of the crew were infected by a mysterious force.**
TRUE/FALSE

6. **The infected crew members said, "Burn with me."**
TRUE/FALSE

7. **Martha was taken over by the solar force.**
TRUE/FALSE

8. **The Doctor had to freeze her to save her.**
TRUE/FALSE

ANSWERS:

1. False. 2. False. 3. True. 4. False. 5. True. 6. True. 7. False. 8. False.

SCORES:

8-10 Congratulations - Riley Vashtee could use someone like you the next time he has to open 29 password-sealed doors!

5-7 A good try. Did someone drain the power to your brain halfway through the episode?

0-4 Your brain must have been frozen to minus 200 degrees! Take the test again when it's thawed!

SPACE ACE OR GALACTIC THUG?

There are many travellers roaming the universe... some get involved in universal affairs and put wrongs to rights. Others are on their own private missions, sorting stuff out in their own special way. But if YOU were given the chance to roam space, what would you get up to? Try the quiz below and find out!

1. On an alien world, you encounter someone you suspect is up to no good. Do you:

a) Try to find out more, acting as off the wall as possible – playing the fool may catch them off their guard.

b) Act as friendly as possible, maybe flirt a little – try to win their confidence.

c) Ignore them – no one has requested you get involved, so why should you?

2. **In a spaceport, someone approaches you, desperate for your help. Do you:**

a) Listen to them closely, ready to get involved.

b) Buy them a coffee, find out more and if you think you can help, do so.

c) Tell them to consult the local law enforcement agencies on the planet.

3. **As you walk down a dark alley on some distant world, minding your own business, you are threatened by an alien street gang. Do you:**

a) Use your big smile and snappy chatter to defuse the situation.

b) Produce a gun and use it to scare them off.

c) Atomise your attackers.

4. **You are searching for a dangerous criminal who has gone undercover in a large office block – someone who could put untold lives in danger. Do you:**
   a) Sneakily go through the computer records trying to find the likeliest suspects.
   b) Strip down to your vest and swing into the building with a big gun, hoping to scare the criminal out of hiding.
   c) Transport the building to neutral territory and scan all those inside it one by one until you find the criminal.

5. **While out exploring a planet one night, you surprise someone who attacks you, thinking you are an enemy. Do you:**
   a) Escape his grip and assure him that you are not his enemy.
   b) Subdue the sucker with force before he hurts others or himself – then explain he's got his wires crossed.
   c) Execute him and continue on your way.

6. **Which one of the following phrases do you think best sums up your attitude to space exploration?**
   a) The universe is a big place and I want to see it all – and any danger is part of the fun!
   b) Hey, do I look good in this outfit? Then let's hit every trouble spot we can find and have some fun!
   c) Do not hinder me while I go about my business, or justice will be swift and deadly.

ANSWERS:

MOSTLY As

You have a bright and breezy attitude to space exploration – much like the Doctor, in fact. You're always ready to believe the best of people until you're proved wrong, and would rather use your wits than your fists in a tight spot. In fact, as you go about your travels through this big, bad universe, someone as self-confident as you will soon be surrounded by troubled souls in need of your help. If you are sure you want to live your life solving other people's problems, that's just fine – but remember that if you get things wrong, it's not just your own life you may be endangering...

MOSTLY Bs

You're an extrovert, and enjoy acting extravagantly – it stops life from getting dull! In fact, you're a little like Captain Jack in that respect. You have a harder edge than someone like the Doctor – you don't like anyone getting the better of you, and give as good as you get. But you're very much a do-gooder at heart, and if something needs fixing, you're there to take the job – and any glory that might come with it! Just remember one thing – when Captain Jack throws himself into an adventure, he can do so knowing that he is indestructible. You are not – so take care of yourself while you're off on your wild trips around the cosmos!

MOSTLY Cs

Oh dear – your selfish, emotionless approach to life among the stars makes you a force to be reckoned with – but not a very nice person to know! Have you ever thought about putting all that attitude and aggression to slightly better use by signing up for a job with the Judoon? Your skin is clearly already as thick as their leathery hides – and with their no-nonsense approach to justice and general disregard for human life, a thug like you would fit in a treat! Just watch out should you ever meet a threat that's even nastier than you – justice will definitely be swift!

HUMAN NATURE
TRUE OR FALSE?

On the run through time and space, the Doctor is forced to take a decision that will have a huge impact on the residents of a quiet English school... But how much of an impact did the story make on YOU?

1. **To escape being caught by a terrifying alien family, the Doctor turned himself into a human called John Smith.**
   TRUE/FALSE

2. **The Doctor placed his Time Lord essence in a grandfather clock.**
   TRUE/FALSE

3. **He hid himself in a school in the 21st century.**
   TRUE/FALSE

4. **Martha became headteacher of the school.**
   TRUE/FALSE

5. **The aliens wanted the Doctor to fight some monsters for them.**
   TRUE/FALSE

6. They created a scarecrow army.

TRUE/FALSE

7. A woman called Joan fell in love with the Doctor's human self.

TRUE/FALSE

8. The Doctor turned himself back into a Time Lord.

TRUE/FALSE

ANSWERS:

1. True. 2. False. 3. False. 4. False. 5. False. 6. True. 7. True. 8. True.

SCORES

6-8 A score like this demonstrates a superhuman nature!

3-5 There is an old saying that "to err is human" - so well done on proving the old saying right!

0-2 To err this much is not human at all - are you an alien who's never watched telly? Pay more attention next time!

DATA SCAN

The quiz that follows tests your powers of data recall. Read the descriptions below, then see if you can correctly identify each object, place or creature. Keep 'em peeled... and here we go!

1. **The mountains go on forever here, with slopes of deep red grass, and they are capped with snow.**
   a) New Earth.
   b) The Moon.
   c) Gallifrey.

2. **A completely black travel machine encasing a powerful mutant.**
   a) Cassandra.
   b) Dalek Sec.
   c) Dalek Caan.

3. **A gigantic bloated arachnid creature with multiple eyes.**
   a) Donna.
   b) The Lazarus Monster.
   c) The Empress of the Racnoss.

4. A cavernous area filled with transparent shafts of fluid and caskets containing dormant humans waiting to be given new life.

a) The lair of the Empress of the Racnoss.

b) The Cult of Skaro laboratory underneath the Empire State Building.

c) Professor Yana's laboratory.

5. A shape-shifting creature who fed on blood.

a) Plasmavore.

b) Carrionite.

c) Weeping Angel.

6. A small but powerful hand-tool with an illuminating blue tip.

a) Laser spanner.

b) Helmic regulator.

c) Sonic screwdriver.

7. Giant crustaceans that feed on exhaust fumes.

a) Macra.

b) Micro.

c) Sycorax.

8. **Masked robotic creatures in Santa disguises.**

a) Roboforms.

b) Toclafane.

c) Futurekind.

9) **A huge, hideous, scuttling mutation that was once human.**

a) The Master.

b) The Lazarus Creature.

c) A Slab.

10. Towering, tubular spacecraft that descend and take off vertically.

a) Slitheen ship.

b) Racnoss ship.

c) Judoon ship.

ANSWERS:

1. c, 2. b, 3. c, 4. b, 5. a, 6. c, 7. a, 8. a, 9. b, 10. c.

SCORES:

8-10 Your brain has incredible powers of recall... you could probably take this test again without once looking at the page!

4-7 There seems to be a bug in your data retrieval system. Hopefully it won't mutate into anything nastier!

0-3 Are you sure you would recognise yourself if you saw your reflection in a mirror?! Don't let life pass you by – look all about you as you go!

BLINK
TRUE OR FALSE?

Trapped in the past, the Doctor's only chance of escape lies with Sally Sparrow – who has no idea of the dangers that lie ahead of her as she solves a very creepy mystery... Can YOU solve the mystery of whether the statements below are true or false?

1. **Sally Sparrow first became involved in the mystery at a house called Wester Drumlins.**
   TRUE/FALSE
2. **Sally's best friend Kathy was touched by a living statue.**
   TRUE/FALSE
3. **The Weeping Angel sent her to the future.**
   TRUE/FALSE
4. **If you so much as blink, a Weeping Angel can sneak up on you.**
   TRUE/FALSE
5. **The Doctor and Martha were touched by a Weeping Angel.**
   TRUE/FALSE

6. The Doctor sent messages to Sally over her mobile phone.

TRUE/FALSE

7. He wanted her to blow up the Weeping Angels with dynamite.

TRUE/FALSE

8. Martha got away from the Weeping Angels and helped Sally fight them.

TRUE/FALSE

ANSWERS:

1. True. 2. True. 3. False. 4. True.
5. True. 6. False. 7. False. 8. False.

SCORES

6-8 You can tell what's true and false in the blink of an eye. Well done!

3-5 Hmm, did you blink and miss some of the action?

0-2 Oh dear - looks like you blinked but then forgot to open your eyes again! Perhaps a Weeping Angel will send you back in time to when the episode was first shown and you can do better next time!

ODD ONE OUT

In each of the groupings below there is an odd one out... Find them, take them down to minus 200 degrees and freeze them out!

1. Dolly Bailey, Lynley, Tish, Peter Streete.

2. Scannell, McDonnell, Riley, Lady Thaw.

3. Brannigan and Valerie, Lucy and the Master, Joan and John Smith, Tallulah and Laszlo the pig slave.

4. Reindeer, Christmas tree decorations, Santa Claus.

5. Francine Jones, Chantho, Lucy.

6. Earth, Malcassairo, Barcelona (the planet), New Earth.

ANSWERS:

1. Tish - the others all knew Shakespeare.

2. Lady Thaw - the others were all crew members of SS Pentallian.

3. Joan and John Smith - they are the only all-human couple.

4. Reindeer - the others were used as weapons by the Empress of the Racnoss.

5. Francine Jones - the others caused the Master to regenerate.

6. Barcelona - we have not seen the TARDIS visit there.

SCORES

5-6 Your fierce intellect and razor-sharp mind must often mark YOU as the odd one out in your crowd!

3-4 It's an 'odd one out' quiz and you got the odd one wrong — but this is still a fine score.

0-2 What a terrible result - you are the very odd one out! Better luck next time...

MONSTER MATCH

This quiz is quite straightforward – match the monsters to the place in which the Doctor and Martha first encountered them!

1. Where did Martha first meet a Slab?

a) In a spaceship.

b) In a hospital.

c) Outside a hospital.

2. Where were the Carrionites hiding?

a) London in the time of Queen Elizabeth I.

b) London in the time of King James I.

c) Scotland in the time of Queen Victoria.

3. Where did Martha meet the Daleks for the first time?

a) The sewers of New York.

b) The streets of London.

c) Hooverville.

4. Where did the Family of Blood pursue the TARDIS to?

a) 19th century Greece.

b) 20th century England.

c) 21st century England.

5. Where did Martha first meet the Master?

a) In a chip shop.

b) On a planet one hundred trillion years in the future.

c) On Earth.

6. Where did the Doctor first encounter the Empress of the Racnoss?

a) In a secret lab beneath the Thames.

b) At Donna Noble's wedding reception.

c) In her spaceship.

7. Where did the Doctor and Martha come up against the so-called Toclafane?

a) On Earth.

b) On Utopia.

c) On Malcassairo.

8. Where did Martha first come up against the crushing claws of the Macra?

a) In a hospital on New Earth.

b) In a spaceship.

c) In the Undercity of New Earth.

ANSWERS

1. c, 2. a, 3. a, 4. b, 5. b, 6. a, 7. a, 8. c.

SCORES

7-8 You have a masterly knowledge of the Doctor and Martha's fearsome foes - congratulations!

3-6 This is a mildly villainous score - but you've got a long way to go before you become truly monstrous.

0-2 Your lack of knowledge is scarier than most monsters - pay attention! Next time Earth is invaded, the Doctor may not be around!

UTOPIA

The Doctor's unexpected visit to the ends of time led to a meeting with an equally unexpected old enemy... But will you be expecting these questions? Take this true or false test and find out!

1. **The Doctor and Martha were visiting Glasgow to refuel the TARDIS.**
   TRUE/FALSE

2. **Captain Jack was invited on-board the TARDIS to join them on their travels.**
   TRUE/FALSE

3. **The Doctor took his friends one hundred trillion years into the future to pick up some milk.**
   TRUE/FALSE

4. **The last humans alive were trying to build a giant statue.**
   TRUE/FALSE

5. **The TARDIS crew found Professor Yana living with a purple baboon.**
   TRUE/FALSE

6. **The last humans were being attacked by the savage Futurekind.**
   TRUE/FALSE

7. The Doctor and his friends helped the last humans escape in a huge rocket.

TRUE/FALSE

8. Professor Yana was secretly a Cyberman in disguise.

TRUE/FALSE

ANSWERS:

1. False. 2. False. 3. False. 4. False.
5. False. 6. True. 7. True. 8. False.

SCORES

6-8 A near perfect score. Quiz book Utopia!

3-5 Hmm - you're a long rocket journey short of a really fabulous score, but you may yet leave the ground.

0-2 A brilliant score - if you are a feeble-minded Futurekind!

AGE ALONE

Using your powers of skill and judgement, rank these characters in order of age – the oldest first, all the way down to the youngest.

1. Martha.
2. The Doctor.
3. Captain Jack.
4. Richard Lazarus.
5. Leo.
6. Latimer.
7. Francine.

ANSWERS:

2, 3, 4, 7, 1, 5, 6.

SCORES:

6 or more correct: Well done - you have great powers of reasoning, whatever your age!

3-5 correct: Not to worry - perhaps as you grow older your skills may improve.

0-2 correct: You have the mental agility of a sleeping Judoon. Perhaps tomorrow you will have woken up and can take the test again!

TIME LORD DRUMMING
TRUE OR FALSE?

Da-da-da-DUMM, da-da-da-DUMM... Is that the sound of distant drums, or the delusions of a man who is the Doctor's greatest enemy? Take the final true or false test and see how much you remember...

1. **The Master was pretending to be a politician called Harold Saxon.**
   TRUE/FALSE
2. **Martha's family were kidnapped on the Master's orders.**
   TRUE/FALSE
3. **The Master made his base on-board an experimental aircraft carrier.**
   TRUE/FALSE
4. **He tried to stop the Toclafane from invading Earth.**
   TRUE/FALSE
5. **The Toclafane were aliens from the planet Toclafanos.**
   TRUE/FALSE
6. **The Master made the Doctor much older.**
   TRUE/FALSE

7. Captain Jack escaped the Master and travelled the world in search of a weapon to use against him.

TRUE/FALSE

8. The Master wanted to rebuild thirteen new Gallifreys in orbit around Earth.

TRUE/FALSE

ANSWERS:

1. True. 2. True. 3. True. 4. False. 5. False. 6. True. 7. False. 8. False.

SCORES

6-8 A great result, but not a surprising one — how could you forget any of the incredible action in this tale of two Time Lords?

3-5 Maybe the Archangel satellites were interfering with your memory of events?

0-2 Er, did you remember to switch your TV set on for these episodes?

THE MEGA CHALLENGE

No perception filter can disguise the fact that this final quiz is the toughest of all – perhaps the ultimate test of your Doctor Who knowledge. The questions have been specially designed to separate the Time Lords from the humans – and if you want to make it even tougher, set yourself a three-minute time limit for all 30 questions!

On your marks... get set... GO!

1. As the Doctor says, "Any number that reduces to 1 when you take the sum of the squares of its digits and continue iterating until it yields one, or produces an infinite loop," is what?

a) Incomprehensible.

b) Infinite.

c) A happy prime.

2. According to the Doctor, what tool did he once own until a "cheeky woman" took it from him?

a) The sonic screwdriver.

b) An etheric beam locator.

c) A laser spanner.

3. What were the first words Sally Sparrow saw on the walls of Wester Drumlins House?

a) Beware the Weeping Angel.

b) What are you looking at?

c) Watch out – there's a statue about.

4. What does Chantho enjoy drinking in Professor Yana's lab?

a) Coffee.

b) Her own internal milk.

c) Human tear-water.

5. By which grand title was Gallifrey also known?

a) The Silver World.

b) The Shining World of the Seven Systems.

c) The Time Star of the East.

6. Where did Richard Lazarus die?

a) St Paul's Cathedral.

b) An ambulance.

c) Southwark Cathedral.

7. Which organisation created the Utopia Project?

a) The Science Foundation.

b) The Utopia Group.

c) The Brotherhood of Faith.

8. What did the Doctor create for Donna Noble with the help of the TARDIS?

a) A fireworks display.

b) A snow shower.

c) A new husband.

9. What type of radiation were the Daleks planning to use to help create their Human Dalek Hybrid army?

a) Gamma radiation.

b) Gammon radiation.

c) Omega radiation.

10. According to the Doctor, what other forms did the human race take as they went on evolving?

a) Liquid and plasma.

b) Little green men and grey big-headed creatures.

c) Clouds of gas and downloads.

11. What did the Doctor pull out of the TARDIS door after arriving on New Earth with Martha?

a) An umbrella.

b) An arrow.

c) A telephone.

12. Chantho believed herself to be the last survivor of which race?

a) The Malmooth.

b) The Menoptra.

c) The Mizzi-Mizzi.

13. How many components were supposedly needed to complete Martha's make-believe Master-beating weapon?

a) Four.

b) Two.

c) One.

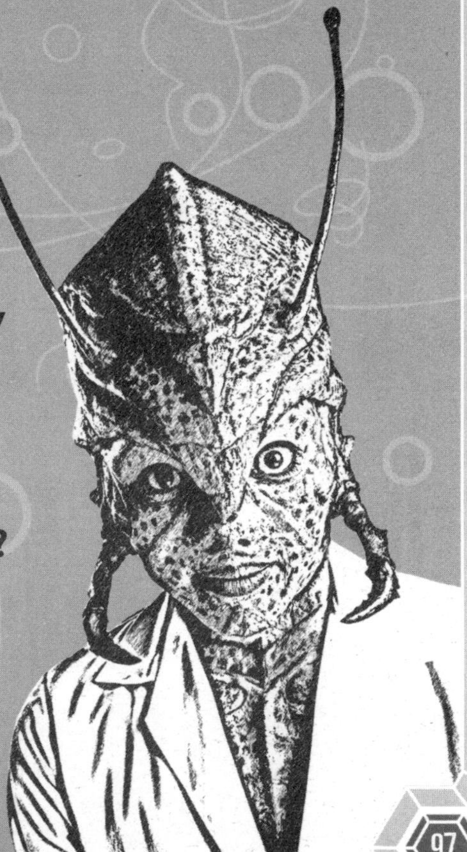

14. The Doctor told Martha that something bad happened whenever he wore which suit?

a) His brown pinstripe suit.

b) His blue pinstripe suit.

c) His dinner suit.

15. Who does Martha call when she needs to know the answer to a security question about pop music on board the SS Pentallian?

a) Her mum.

b) Her brother.

c) Radio One.

16. What did the Doctor use to help disguise himself, Martha and Jack when they were on the run from the Master's henchmen?

a) His fob watch.

b) TARDIS keys.

c) The sonic screwdriver.

17. From which race were the Toclafane descended?

a) The Judoon.

b) The Daleks.

c) Humans.

18. **For how long was New Earth placed in quarantine following the virus outbreak that devastated the planet?**
   a) Ten years.
   b) 100 years.
   c) 500 years.

19. **In which part of London was Donna Noble to be married?**
   a) Brentford.
   b) Ealing.
   c) Chiswick.

20. **How many satellites made up the Master's Archangel network?**
   a) Three.
   b) Fifteen.
   c) Two hundred.

21. What was the surname of Sally Sparrow's best friend, Kathy?

a) Nightingale.

b) Swallow.

c) Starfish.

22. When the Doctor seemed to kiss Martha on the moon, what was he really up to?

a) Lip-to-lip cell renewal.

b) A genetic transfer.

c) A lipisome transmutation.

23. How many Toclafane made up the Master's invasion force?

a) One million.

b) Ten million.

c) Six billion.

24. Where did the Doctor discover a Dalek embryo abandoned to die?

a) In the sewers of New York.

b) In Hooverville.

c) In the Empire State Building.

25. Who originally found the words to banish the Carrionites from the universe?

a) The Master.

b) The Eternals.

c) The Judoon.

26. Who ordered the Empress of the Racnoss's spaceship to be shot out of the sky?

a) Torchwood.

b) Mr Saxon.

c) Donna Noble's mum.

27. When the Doctor was asked if he had a brother, what was his reply?

a) "Not any more."

b) "Yes, two."

c) "Can I have a cup of tea?"

28. What did Captain Jack use as a "Doctor Detector"?

a) A tracking device.

b) A piece of the Doctor's skin gouged from a Slitheen claw.

c) The Doctor's own hand, which he lost in a Sycorax swordfight soon after regenerating.

29. When the Lazarus creature activated the machine that had spawned it in an effort to kill the Doctor and Martha, how was it defeated?

a) Martha stunned it with a supersonic scream.

b) The Doctor electrocuted it.

c) The Doctor reversed the polarity of the device.

30. What was marked on the sliding door that concealed the Empress of the Racnoss's shaft to the centre of the Earth?

a) LAB 003.

b) WARNING — STEEP DROP AHEAD.

c) EMERGENCY EXIT.

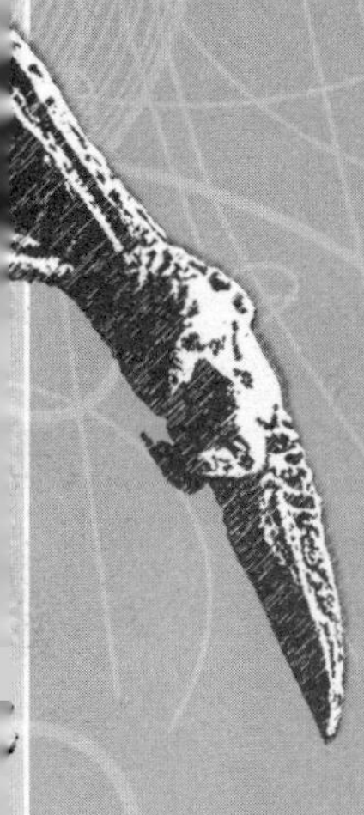

ANSWERS:

1. c, 2. c, 3. a, 4. b, 5. b, 6. c, 7. a, 8. b, 9. a, 10. c, 11. b, 12. a 13. a, 14. c, 15. a, 16. b, 17. c, 18. b, 19. c, 20. b, 21. a, 22. b, 23. c, 24. a, 25. b, 26. b, 27. a, 28. c, 29. c, 30. a.

SCORE:

26-30 OH, YES! A spectacular display of Doctor Who expertise! You are a true fan.

22-25 A few slips, granted - but this is still a splendid result and one you can be proud of.

17-21 You know a fair bit about the Doctor and his adventures, but you're not yet a devoted fan.

10-16 Hmm - a ravenous Futurekind might be proud of this result, but few others would be!

5-9 Even a ravenous Futurekind would hang his head in shame at this result!

0-4 Has your brain been fried by a runaway MRI unit? Get well soon... and watch all the Doctor's adventures again while you're recovering!

CHECK OUT THESE OTHER EXCITING DOCTOR WHO BOOKS: